To Vincent B.

Thank you to Claudia Berger, Lecturer in Chinese Studies
at the University of Geneva, for her kind collaboration.

First published in France by Editions Philippe Picquier under the title *La naissance du DRAGON*.
Published in the United States, Great Britain, Canada, Australia, and New Zealand in 2007 by
North-South Books Inc., an imprint of NordSüd Verlag AG, Zürich, Switzerland.

Distributed in the United States by North-South Books Inc., New York.

Library of Congress Cataloging-in-Publication Data is available.
A CIP catalogue record for this book is available from The British Library.

ISBN 978-0-7358-2152-1 (trade edition)
10 9 8 7 6 5 4 3 2

Printed in China

www.northsouth.com

Legend of the Chinese
DRAGON

Written by Marie Sellier
Illustrated by Catherine Louis
Calligraphy and chop marks by
Wang Fei
Translated by Sibylle Kazeroid

NorthSouth
New York / London

Once upon a time, long, long ago,
the men, women, and children of China
hunted, fished, and lived in tribes under
the protection of benevolent spirits.

上古時代，龍還沒有出現，部落居民漁獵為生，信奉不同的圖騰

These spirits resembled the animals
with which they had always lived.

Those near the ocean had chosen
the spirit of the fish, which glistens
in the water.

魚

近水部落信奉魚魚是
他們賴以生存的食物

鳥

高山部落信奉鳥

它可以搏擊雲天

Those in the mountains
had adopted the bird,
which is good at chasing
clouds away.

Those in the low plains
preferred the horse, which
gallops as fast as the wind.

平原部落信奉

馬它追風逐電

Those in the high plains put themselves under the protection of the serpent, which glides silently from one place to another.

蛇

高原部落信奉
蛇它舒捲自如
又悄無聲息

牛

耕作部落信奉牛它既是人類
的朋友同時又勞作不息

Those in the fertile rice fields
swore by the ox, friend of man
and tireless worker.

In this way, the men, women, and children of China lived, each tribe under the protection of the fish, or the bird, or the horse, or the serpent, or the ox.

Sadly, the tribes were envious of one another, and often waged war among themselves in the names of their spirits.

爭

各部落生活在魚鳥馬蛇牛諸圖騰
的保護下又以圖騰的名義進行戰爭

They fought so much that
one day the children of all
the tribes of China decided
that they had enough of fighting
and declared war on war.

騰它敏捷如魚自由似鳥迅疾若馬聰明比蛇力大像牛

孩子們厭倦了戰爭他們要創造出一個新的圖

They decided to create an animal that would protect *all* the people: an animal that was agile like the fish, free like the bird, fast like the horse, cunning like the serpent, and strong like the ox.

So, they took the body of the serpent and glued to it the scales of the fish. They took the head of the horse and attached the horns of the ox. Then they attached the head to the body, and added the wings of the bird.

新圖騰有蛇的身體魚的
鱗甲馬的頭部牛的雙角
鳥的利爪

龍

新圖騰可以上天入地潛水

它的名字叫龍

They called this fabulous
animal—which could fly
in the air, swim in the ocean,
and walk on land—DRAGON.

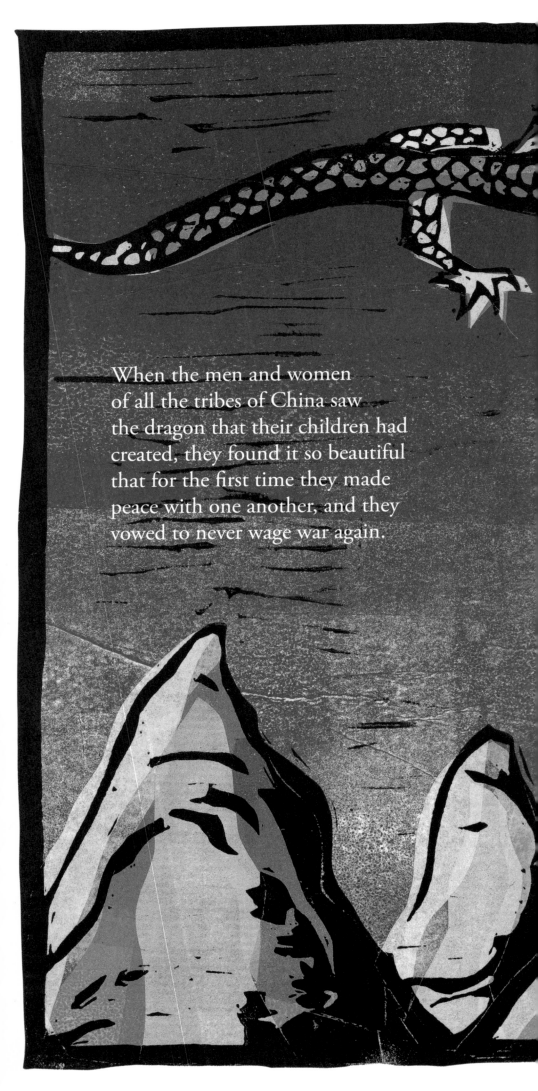

When the men and women
of all the tribes of China saw
the dragon that their children had
created, they found it so beautiful
that for the first time they made
peace with one another, and they
vowed to never wage war again.

大家對孩子們的龍讚賞

有加一致同意奉龍

為統一的圖騰停止戰爭

They didn't always succeed, and there were wars over the years. But the dragon still remains a symbol of peace, and plays an important role at Chinese celebrations.

此後的歲月盡管還有戰爭但龍一直保留了下來成了祥和的象徵每年春節都舞龍慶賀

Marie Sellier loves to talk to children about art. But what she loves best is writing children's books, which bring art to life.

In her life and in her work, China has had an enormous influence on **Catherine Louis.** Although she lives in Switzerland, a small piece of her heart has moved far away to the land of the dragon. Louis is also the author and illustrator of *Liu and the Bird: A Journey in Chinese Calligraphy* published by North-South Books Inc.

Wang Fei grew up in China, where he learned Chinese calligraphy. He believes that the present comes from both the past and the future, and he looks for the road in between.